THE THREE LITTLE ALIENS AND THE BIG BAD ROBOT

SATURN

URANUS

NEPTUNE

For my three little siblings,
because we always stick together —M.M.

For Lily, my little alien —M.F.

ISBN 978-0-545-94878-4

12 11 10 9 8 7 6 5 4 3 2 1   16 17 18 19 20 21

Printed in the U.S.A.   40

First Scholastic printing, January 2016

The text of this book is set in New Clear Era.

The illustrations were drawn by hand and rendered digitally using collage techniques.

Book design by Rachael Cole and Erin Supinski

THE THREE LITTLE ALIENS AND THE BIG BAD ROBOT

written by MARGARET McNAMARA • illustrated by MARK FEARING

SCHOLASTIC INC.

Once there was a mama alien who had three little aliens.

They were called Bork, Gork, and Nklxwcyz.

Bork, Gork, and Nklxwcyz grew up in an old-fashioned house in a snug, cozy crater on a tiny little planet.

As the eons passed, their house got too crowded.

"It's time for you to go out into the universe and find a planet of your own," their mama told them, giving each a hug. "But remember: watch out for the Big Bad Robot. It wants to chew you up."

So Bork, Gork, and Nklxwcyz took off.

"Bye, Mama!" they cried.

"Bye, kids!" she shouted back. "Always stick together," she added. Then she sniffed a little bit. "And call me every once in a while."

The three little aliens traveled far and fast.

"There's a cute planet," said Bork.

"Too hot," said Nklxwcyz.

"How about that one?" asked Gork.

"Too crowded," replied Nklxwcyz.

They darted around a meteor.

"Are we there yet?" asked Bork.

Just past the next bend, a big planet, swirling with dust, loomed into view. Bork spotted a shiny space rover zipping around its mountains and plains. "Awesome!" she said. "I'm going to live in that."

"Ma said to stick together," called Nklxwcyz.

But Bork had already zipped too far away to hear.

Nklxwcyz and Gork traveled on. Nklxwcyz didn't
like the looks of the next planet, either. "Nowhere to
breathe," he gasped.

"Picky, picky," Gork said. Then, just ahead, he
spied a giant planet with huge golden rings around it.

He jumped on a passing satellite and caught a ride on a ring. "Whee!" he squealed. "This is what I call home!"

"We can't live on a ring that goes around in circles," yelled Nklxwcyz. "We'll get dizzy!"

But Gork wasn't paying any attention.

Now Nklxwcyz was all alone. He traveled deeper and deeper into space until he spotted a massive blue planet, far out in the galaxy. It had thirteen moons, and refreshing breezes.

"This faraway place is where I'll build my home,"
he said. "It will be safe from the Big Bad Robot."

Nklxwcyz found everything
he needed to make sturdy walls.

He gathered stardust to keep his
home bright and found solar panels
to keep it warm.

Then he grabbed a tall, shiny
telescope. "This'll do for a chimney,"
he said, though no one heard him.

Rock by rock and row by row, Nklxwcyz built the perfect house. When he was finished, he sat down and locked the door.

His house was not very zippy or cool, but it was very safe. And there was room enough for all three little aliens.

"I hope they come to visit soon," said Nklxwcyz.

Then, one galactic dawn, there
was a rumbling in the universe.

GREEP
BOINK

MEEP
PEEEDILY
DEEEP
ORK
EEP

It was the Big Bad Robot!

Bork was so busy on her swirly red planet that she couldn't hear the Robot's call. She didn't feel its giant footsteps as it leapt from star to star.

And she didn't see the Robot . . .

... until it was right in front of her rover!

"Little alien! Little alien!" bleeped the Robot. "Pull over! PULL OVER!"

"Not by the wheels of my trusty space rover!" cried Bork bravely.

"Then I'll crack and smack and whack your house down!" meeped the Robot.

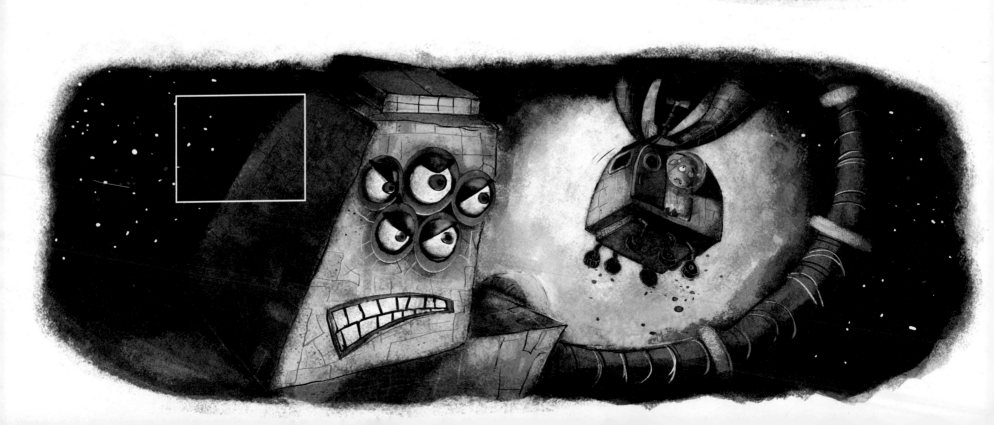

And just like that, the Robot cracked and
smacked and whacked Bork's shiny rover into
a hundred pieces!

GREEP
BOINK
MEEP

PEEDILY
DEEP ORK
EEP EEP

As fast as the speed of sound, Bork jetted
away, the Robot close behind her. Just as the
Robot was about to eat her up, she spotted
Gork's satellite house.

"Gork! Gork! Help me!" she cried.

But Gork was having so much fun surfing on the
rings of his giant planet that he didn't hear Bork's
cries. He didn't see the Robot chomping on comets
and ripping open black holes . . . until the Big Bad
Robot caught Gork's satellite in his huge metal claw.

"Little alien! Little alien!" it broinked. "COME OUT OF HIDING!"

"Not by the orbit of this ring I'm riding!" cried Gork stoutly.

"Then I will shatter and clatter and scatter your house down!" groinked the Robot.

And before Gork could fly beneath the
radar, that Robot clattered and scattered and
shattered Gork's satellite into a thousand
pieces.

GREEP

BOINK

ORK

M

DE

EEP

PEEEDILY

E

Gork barely escaped. "Over here!" called Bork. "Stick together!"

At the speed of light, Bork and Gork blasted out into space, with the Big Bad Robot getting closer all the time.

"Where can we hide?" asked Gork.

"Let's find Nklxwcyz!" cried Bork.

"He'll know what to do."

Nklxwcyz had heard the Robot's roar. He had seen what was going on with his brother and sister through his telescope. And he was ready.

He flashed his solar panels halfway across the universe.

"There he is!" cried Bork and Gork. And they zoomed to Nklxwcyz's house as fast as a hurtling asteroid.

"Get inside!" cried Nklxwcyz. "No time to waste!"

No sooner had Bork and Gork slammed Nklxwcyz's solid space-rock door than they heard the Robot rumbling.
"Little alien! Little alien!" he queeked.

"LET ME COME IN!"

"Not by the slime on my chinny chin chin!" cried Nklxwcyz.

"Then I will smack and crack and whack your house down!" zeeped the Robot.

The Big Bad Robot bashed and
crashed Nklxwcyz's strong, solid house.
Nothing happened.

Then it pounded and
smashed. Really hard.
Not a crack.

Then it loaded up its triple blaster
and zapped that house but good.
That house would not fall down.

So the Robot forced its way into the little alien's house, right down the chimney!

GREEEEEEEP BA-DEEEEEEEP

The aliens covered their ears and waited for the Robot to chomp them up.

But halfway down the telescope, that Robot got stuck tight.

It strained and it struggled. It moaned and it groaned.

Nklxwcyz's house shook and shuddered, but did it fall down?

It did not!

The Robot gave one more mighty cry and burst into a

million pieces!

"Cool," said Bork.

"Awesome," said Gork.

"Just as I planned," said Nklxwcyz.

"There's just one thing missing," said Bork.

"Phone home," said Gork.

So Nklxwcyz did.

"Ma," he said, "we have the coziest house in the galaxy. Won't you come over and tuck us in?"

And she did.

AUTHOR'S NOTE

This book is not a science book, but there is a little bit of science in the aliens' travels. The aliens and their mama live on Mercury, the smallest planet, which is closest to the sun. When the aliens leave home, they pass all the other planets in our solar system, in order of the planets' distance from the sun. They start by zipping past Venus, which is the brightest planet in our night sky. Next they pass Earth, our home, the watery blue planet; and after that comes Mars, the red planet. Then the two alien brothers fly by the fifth planet from the sun, Jupiter, which is made of gases, and come to Saturn, with its glorious rings. The last little alien passes Uranus, whose atmosphere is icy, and finally settles on Neptune (where winds blow as fast as 1,290 miles per hour!), the farthest planet from the sun.

Mark Fearing researched the planets so that he could depict them as accurately as possible, and based their coloration on photographs provided by NASA. All eight planets are shown on the endpapers, though the distance between them is not to scale. For more information about our solar system, visit www.nasa.gov.